j91-547

Hughes, Dean

Superstar team

$6.99   5/91

DATE		
AUG 2 1 1991	AUG 1 0 1994	
NOV 3 0 1991	SEP 2 1 1994	
MAY 1 1 1992	APR 2 6 1995	
JUL 2 1992	JUL 1 9 1995	
JUL 1 1 1992		
JUL 3 0 1992		
JUN 1 0 1993		
JUL 1 4 1994		
AUG 4		

© THE BAKER & TAYLOR CO.

Ben was running back for the ball, and Anthony came charging in.

But neither one called for it, and both kept running. And then Anthony and Ben, both at the same time, decided to let the other one make the catch.

The ball dropped between them.

The run scored.

And Jonathan lost his shutout.

"You stupid *idiots!*" he screamed.

*Look for these books about the
Angel Park All-Stars*

SUPERSTAR TEAM

By Dean Hughes

Illustrated by Dennis Lyall

Bullseye Books • Alfred A. Knopf
New York

Library of Congress Cataloging-in-Publication Data
Hughes, Dean, 1943–
Superstar team / by Dean Hughes ; illustrated by Dennis Lyall.
p.   cm.—(Angel Park all-stars ; 9)
Summary: Follows the members of the Angel Park Dodgers Little
League team through their second season as they discuss batting
averages, RBIs, and Jonathan Swingle, the new superstar and super
braggart.
ISBN 0-679-81536-8 (pbk.)—ISBN 0-679-91536-2 (lib. bdg.)
[1. Baseball—Fiction. I. Lyall, Dennis, ill. II. Title.
III. Series: Hughes, Dean, 1943–   Angel Park all-stars ; 9.
PZ7.H87312Su   1991
[Fic]—dc20   90-53314

RL: 4.5
First Bullseye Books edition: April 1991
Manufactured in the United States of America
10 9 8 7 6 5 4 3 2 1

for Kathy Kendell

★ 1 ★

Big Talk

Kenny Sandoval sprinted for third and slid hard. He beat the throw by a mile.

"Good slide," Coach Wilkens said. He slapped Kenny on the back. "Did all you kids see how he did that?"

This was the first practice of the year, and the coach was working on basics. He was having the Dodger players watch as each one took a turn sliding into third.

Kenny smiled as he walked over to his friends Jacob Scott and Harlan Sloan. He was glad the coach liked his slide.

"I swear you're getting faster," Jacob said. "You were *flying*."

"Kenny, one thing to remember," the coach said. "When you make the turn at second, always tag the bag with your right foot. That helps you cut that corner."

Jacob, a freckle-faced kid, was grinning, showing the split between his front teeth. "As fast as Kenny is, it doesn't matter," he said.

But the coach heard that. "That's not true, Jacob. There's a right way to do things—no matter how fast a player is."

Next to go was the new kid, Jonathan Swingle. He was standing at first base with his hands on his hips. The kid was a giant for a fifth grader.

Michael Wilkens, the coach's son and this year's assistant coach, tossed the ball in the air and then stroked a line drive to right field. Jonathan took off.

Like a *rocket!*

Sterling Malone charged the ball, took it on one bounce and threw hard to third.

But Jonathan made a perfect turn at second, raced toward third, and dove in head first. Henry White fielded the ball on one hop and slammed his glove down for the tag.

But too late!

Jonathan's hand was already on the bag.

"Wow!" Harlan yelled. He turned to Kenny. "I thought *you* were fast. Jonathan runs like *Bo Jackson!*"

Kenny was impressed, too. But then Jacob said, "The guy is going to be a *superstar!*" Kenny tried not to let that bother him. But the truth was, he had sort of expected to be the star himself this year.

All day it had been the same thing. Everyone was talking about Jonathan.

At batting practice Jonathan had filled the air with line drives. And he had played infield like a major-leaguer. On top of that, the guy was a pitcher, and he could throw *smoke*.

Kenny was glad to have him on the team; he was going to give the Dodgers just what they needed to be really tough this year. Still, Jacob didn't have to start calling him a "superstar."

And Jacob wasn't the only one thinking that way. Billy Bacon yelled, *"Nobody* is going to stop the Dodgers this year! Jonathan's a one-man team."

"We'll *kill* the Giants and the Reds!" Eddie Boschi shouted.

Most of the players barked, *"YEAH!!!"*

But Kenny didn't say anything. All this talk bothered him. The team sounded too much like the cocky Reds that Eddie was so sure they could beat.

Coach Wilkens asked everyone to quiet down. "Before you brag too much," he said, "let's make sure we get the basics right. I want you to notice a couple of things. Sterling charged the ball just right, but then he stopped before he threw the ball. By doing that, he lost power on his throw."

Coach Wilkens had to wait when he noticed some of the kids talking, not paying attention.

Then he went on. "I don't want you sliding head first. It's too easy to get hurt. And when you slide, keep your fists doubled," he said. "That way you don't jamb your fingers."

The next runner getting ready to try his slide was one of the rookies, Ben Riddle.

The bat pinged and Ben took off.

Sort of.

His legs pumped and his arms waved—but he wasn't getting anywhere. He was lucky that Anthony Ruiz, the other nine-year-old on this year's team, was fielding the ball in right field.

Anthony bumbled forward and stuck his glove out, but the ball hopped up and hit him in the shoulder. It glanced away, and he had to chase it.

The race was on. The turtle against . . . the turtle.

Everyone was laughing, even Jacob and Harlan—and Kenny—last year's rookies.

Anthony finally got hold of the ball and looped a throw toward third. Henry had to leave the bag to catch the ball, and Ben got by him. But his slide was late and awkward.

"Don't break a leg off, Ben," Jonathan yelled. "You're slow enough with two."

Everyone laughed. Jenny Roper did say, "Good job, Ben," and Kenny knew she was trying to make him feel better. But even she was laughing.

Kenny felt bad for the rookies. He remembered how he had felt when he and his friends had been the new guys.

Coach Wilkens showed Ben how to start his slide sooner and how to tuck one leg under as he dropped to the ground.

Jonathan walked over to Billy, the stubby little catcher. Jonathan had moved to the little town of Angel Park during the winter. He and Billy, a sixth grader, had already become good friends.

"The only bad thing is," Jonathan said, "those two little retards are going to be out there playing for us."

Billy chuckled in his low voice. "Maybe we can stick them out in right field, one at a time."

"Yeah, but they have to bat at least once."

"Hey, don't worry," Billy said. "We have so many great hitters on this team, we're going to be ahead by twenty runs before the coach ever puts those guys in the game."

Kenny thought of all the great hitters on the Dodgers' team: Henry White, Jenny Roper, Sterling Malone, Lian Jie. Eddie and Billy had been pretty good last season too, and they were looking even better this year. Jacob and Harlan had also improved last season, and they had practiced a lot since then.

And Kenny? He had been one of the best the year before, even as a third grader. Up until now, all the players had been saying he was going to be the star this year.

"You and Kenny and Henry are probably the best players in the league," Billy said. "And we've got *all three* of you."

Jonathan turned toward Kenny. "What was your batting average last year, Kenny?"

"I don't know exactly," Kenny said.

"I'll bet it was close to .500," Billy said.

"You can't believe all the hits he got. Just think what he'll do this year!"

"I hit .580," Jonathan said. "I had six home runs and 42 runs batted in. Everybody on my team called me *Swat Swingle*."

"Yeah. *SWAT!!*" Billy yelled.

Kenny nodded. He was a soft-spoken boy, but his quiet brown eyes let his confidence show through. "That's good," he said. "Where did you play?"

"In Riverside. They have great teams in the cities around L.A." He laughed. "But I was the best player in the league."

Kenny thought that was probably true. Jonathan had a build like Jose Canseco, and everything he did looked natural. He was a great athlete; anyone could see that.

"I'm going to make the majors. I already made up my mind about that," Jonathan said.

He rolled his shoulders like a body builder. But then he grinned. With his almost white hair and knobby cheeks, he looked like a little kid just happy to be so good. It was hard not to like the guy—even if he was a bragger.

"Hey, Kenny will make it to the majors for sure," Harlan said. "I want to, too, and so does—"

But Jonathan started to laugh. "Don't kid yourself," he said. "It's tough. What did *you* bat last year?"

Harlan shrugged, and then looked at the ground. He was big for his age, but he looked like a weakling next to Jonathan.

Kenny was pretty sure Harlan knew his batting average—and it had been very good by the end of the year. But he wasn't about to admit what it was to a guy who was claiming .580.

But Henry White came to Harlan's rescue. "Harlan improved a lot," he said. "He's going to be really good."

Jonathan smiled and said to Henry, "Billy tells me you're a good hitter too." He sounded as though he wasn't sure he believed it.

"He hit over .500 last year too," Billy said.

"Jenny was almost that high. And Sterling has grown about four inches. He's going to hit some *long* shots this year."

"Hey, I'm glad I moved here," Jonathan said. "We're going to be *great!* Last year you guys won the league championship, but this year I say we can take the district tournament. I've seen some great teams from L.A., but I think we can beat 'em."

"THAT'S RIGHT!!!!" Eddie Boschi yelled, and he waved those long, wild arms of his over his head.

"We're going to *DESTROY* teams!!!" Jonathan yelled.

And everyone cheered. But just then the coach walked over.

"Hey, kids, they don't give the championship to the team that *talks* the best game. They give it to the team that *wins* the most games. Now let's get back to work on some fundamentals."

Kenny was thinking the same thing.

But the Dodgers were going to be good this year. Maybe it wasn't too much to think they could beat the teams in L.A. and win the district championship.

And then Jonathan said, "From what I've seen, there's not a team in the league that will even give us a good game."

It was that kind of talk that worried Kenny. "I don't know," he said. "We can't get overconfident."

"That's not a problem for me. I just know what I can do."

Kenny didn't say anything, but he made up his mind to show this hotshot that he wasn't the only good player on the team.

2

Hot Start

The first game was on a Saturday morning in March.

Baseball started early in the desert towns of Southern California because the summers were so hot. But this day was perfect, warm and calm, with lots of blue sky. And the Angel Park four-diamond complex was all groomed and ready to go.

The Dodgers were playing the Mariners, one of the weaker teams the year before. But the Mariners had brought lots of fans from San Lorenzo, a town like Angel Park that had only one Little League team.

Because the towns were small, kids nine through twelve all played in one league. But the area was known for producing great players. The Mariners had a good team—in a tough league.

The coach had the players sit on the grass, and then he announced the starting lineup.

Jonathan was pitching and batting fourth.

Kenny would be playing shortstop and batting third.

And Jacob was *starting* in right field.

Harlan told Jacob and Kenny, "I don't care that I'm not starting. I knew I probably wouldn't. But the coach told me I'd play a lot. Not just at first but at catcher too."

So the three fourth-grade friends were feeling good.

"Yes, fans," Jacob said in his radio announcer's voice, "it's a great day for baseball. A huge crowd has gathered. But I feel sorry for the poor Mariners. They don't stand a chance against the *superstar* Dodgers."

"Well, Frank," Jacob added, and he switched to a voice with a country twang, "I have to agree with you. These here Dodgers may be the greatest team ever to play Little League baseball."

Jacob nodded to Kenny, and Kenny

smiled, but the coach yelled, "Jacob, let's concentrate on *playing*, okay?"

And that they did.

Lian Jie led off for the Dodgers. The Taiwanese player had learned a lot of English in the last year and had grown enough that he didn't look so small—even if he was still the smallest player on the field.

But he didn't hit small.

The Mariners' pitcher was nervous and had trouble getting the ball over the plate. But when he finally did, Lian slapped it up the middle for a solid single.

"ALL RIGHT!!!!" Billy yelled from the dugout. "That's how the year begins—and *nobody,* but *nobody,* stops us!"

And he seemed to be right.

Henry White didn't get a pitch in the strike zone, but he didn't get anxious. He took the walk.

When Kenny came up, he had his mind made up. He was going to start the season right, and show Jonathan what he could do. He got a fat pitch down the middle, and he *smacked* it.

The ball zinged past the left fielder and bounced to the fence. Both runs scored and Kenny cruised into second with a stand-up double. He loved it!

"Hey," Jonathan yelled to Kenny, "you got two RBIs, and only left one for me. I guess I'll have to bring myself in with a *homer.*"

The coach didn't like that.

The Mariner players didn't like it either. Someone in the dugout yelled, "Just get in the batter's box and shut up!"

But Jonathan was the one who shut some mouths. He drove a fly over the left fielder's head. He came within a few feet of getting the home run he wanted.

Kenny scored, and then, when the left fielder threw the ball over the third baseman's head, Jonathan turned on the juice and went all the way home.

As Jonathan trotted back to the dugout, with the score already four to nothing, he said, "I can't count my score as an RBI. So that puts you one ahead of me. But then . . . I'll catch up next time I bat."

Kenny didn't say anything, but he told himself, "We'll see about that."

"Hey, the whole team's batting a thousand," Eddie Boschi yelled. "Let's keep that stat all season!"

It seemed they could when Sterling and Jenny both hit singles. But then it was Eddie himself who made the first out of the season. He hit a line drive right at the third baseman.

Billy didn't get a hit either, but he bounced a grounder to the right side, and the runners moved up to second and third.

The rally was dying. But then Jacob came through with a hotshot grounder that skipped past the shortstop.

Two more runs scored and the Dodgers were ahead by six before the Mariners had even come to bat.

When Lian flied out, the Dodgers were out of the inning, but they were flying high. They could hardly wait to get out there and mow down the Mariners—and then start scoring all over again.

The poor Mariners looked like they had

already lost the battle. "Come on, hustle in!" their coach yelled to them. "Get your heads up. Let's score some runs."

"Yeah, right," Henry said to Kenny. They both laughed.

Kenny didn't like to make fun of the Mariners, but they had lost their big pitcher, Perez, and their catcher, who had been their best hitter. Kenny didn't think they would give the Dodgers much trouble all season.

As Jacob ran past the mound on his way to right field, he shouted to Jonathan, "Hey, I just caught Kenny for the RBI lead. I got two of my own. We're *both* ahead of you."

"Yeah, well, that won't last long," Jonathan said, and he rolled his big shoulders. He was smiling, but Kenny saw how sure he was of himself.

He stepped onto the rubber, and then with a relaxed motion, fired a warmup pitch to Billy that *popped*, and sent dust flying from the catcher's mitt.

He got the ball back and . . . *POP*.

Every pitch was under control, and *hard*.

The poor kid who finally stepped up to bat, the second baseman, looked scared. He was short and fairly quick, a good lead-off batter—if he could get some wood on the ball. But that didn't seem likely.

When he let the first pitch go by—right down the middle—Kenny knew he was hoping for a walk.

POP.

The kid swung very late.

POP.

That was that.

Jonathan laughed. When the throw from Billy came back, it bounced and glanced off Jonathan's glove. He had to run toward shortstop to get it.

He looked at Kenny and said, "I've got a perfect game going."

Kenny nodded and he caught himself laughing. His dad had always told him not to act like that. But maybe it wasn't so bad. Maybe Jonathan's confidence would spread to the whole team. Maybe Kenny needed more of that himself.

"I almost pitched a perfect game last year," Jonathan said. "I would have, too, but this dumb kid on our team made an error. But I still got a no-hitter."

"Jonathan," Coach Wilkens yelled, "play ball."

Jonathan did. He struck out the next batter on three pitches again. A foul tip was the best the batter could manage.

And then Jonathan did a job on the Mariners' best hitter—a guy named Cast, the center fielder. Jonathan set him up with an inside pitch, and then came with a heater on the outside corner.

Cast reached for it and fouled it off. Still, he had timed Jonathan's fast ball pretty well.

But Jonathan had a change-up that he knew how to control. He gave the pitch his big motion and the ball just . . . floated.

Cast tried to stop his swing, but he popped the ball up on the infield. Jonathan ran toward first and took the pop-up himself even though it should have been Jenny's catch.

"All right!" Jonathan yelled. "Five more innings. I'm going to get my perfect game today."

Coach Wilkens wanted to talk to Jonathan when he came back to the dugout. Kenny didn't hear what the coach said, but Kenny knew what Coach Wilkens thought of the stuff Jonathan was saying.

Jonathan's head nodded a few times, as though he were taking it all to heart. But when he walked into the dugout he whispered to Kenny. "Perfect game. Just watch me."

Kenny didn't know what to think of the guy. He acted like such a hotshot, and yet, Kenny sort of liked him. He probably *would* pitch a perfect game—or anything else he wanted to do.

But maybe Kenny would show him that he wasn't the only good player around. Maybe Kenny would hang on to that RBI lead. In fact, he *promised* himself he would do it.

3

Less than Perfect

The Dodgers picked up a couple more runs in the second inning. But "Swat" missed his chance to drive in two runs when he swung for the fence and lifted an easy fly to left field.

When Jonathan saw that the left fielder was going to catch the ball, he slammed his bat on the ground. Kenny was surprised that he was quite *that* upset. No one could get a hit every time at bat—not even Jonathan.

Sterling Malone, the Dodgers' powerful center fielder, used his head and took a nice, even stroke and drove in the runs.

Kenny crossed the plate and headed for

the dugout. Jonathan didn't cheer. He turned to Billy just as Kenny entered the dugout, and he said, "Those should have been *my* RBIs."

Everyone was yelling for Jenny to get a hit, but Jonathan said, "That guy pitches so slow it's hard to time him. I'm used to pitchers who are almost as good as I am."

"Don't worry about it," Billy said. "We'll beat these guys easy."

"Hey, I'm not worried about that," Jonathan said. "But I don't want to ruin my stats in the first game." He glanced over at Kenny, who had gotten his second hit. "I'm not going to let myself get behind a *fourth* grader."

He smiled. But he seemed to be forcing himself this time.

Kenny didn't like that. If Jonathan wanted a hitting contest, Kenny could give him all he could handle. Confidence was one thing, but this guy wanted *all* the glory.

When Jonathan hustled back to the

mound, he seemed in a hurry to get the Mariners out.

But he didn't wipe out the Mariners quite so easily as he expected. The tall first base- man, Rodriguez, led off the inning. He didn't have a great swing, but he got the bat on the ball and blooped it into right field.

Jonathan was furious. He yelled to Rodriguez, "You just lucked out, kid!"

Kenny heard Jonathan's parents yelling the same thing. "Hey, try swinging," Jonathan's dad bellowed. "I think you shut your eyes and stuck out the bat."

His mother was hollering, "Don't worry, Jonny. You'll still shut them out."

Some of the Mariners' fans didn't like that. They yelled for their team to knock that "cocky kid" off the mound.

Jonathan did get the next two batters, but he tried to be a bit too fancy, and he walked the right fielder.

He got fired up then, and he popped in three strikes so hard that the batter just stood there and watched them go by. Then he slammed his fist in his glove and walked off the mound. "Don't even *think* about getting a run today!" he yelled to the Mariners.

Jonathan looked over at Kenny. That big knobby-cheeked grin was back. But Kenny was sort of bothered. Maybe he didn't like the guy so much after all.

Billy was up first in the top of the third. He took a good swing, but the ball was in on his knees, and he squibbed it out to the pitcher.

And then Jacob went for a pitch that was actually high. He popped it up.

The Mariners' pitcher didn't throw hard, but he was starting to move the ball around better, and his control was coming along.

Lian did a better job of staying with the off-speed pitches. He punched the ball into center for his second hit.

But Henry found himself lunging at a slow pitch and grounding it to second base for out number three.

Jonathan yelled, "Come on, you guys. I can't drive in runs if no one gets on."

The coach had begun to change the Dodgers' defense. Harlan Sloan was getting the catcher's gear on. Anthony Ruiz was running out to play right field. And little Ben Riddle was going in for Lian at second.

Jonathan marched out to the mound, but he suddenly stopped and looked at Kenny. "Oh, great," he said. "With these guys in the game I'll have to strike everybody out. I don't dare let 'em hit the ball."

Michael Wilkens yelled from the first-base coach's box, "Hey, Jonathan, no more of that."

Kenny knew what Michael meant. He trotted over to the mound. Jonathan had just thrown a hard warmup pitch, and he was waiting for Harlan to throw it back. He caught the ball and then looked over at Kenny.

"Jonathan," Kenny said, "the young guys are playing for the first time, and—"

"Yeah, I don't see why the coach has to put all the benchwarmers in at the same time."

"They need the experience. Harlan is learning how to catch, and he—"

"Learning how? Are you kidding? Let him learn at practice. We don't need him messing up in games."

"We've got a big lead and this is a good chance for him to get some game experience. The same with the third graders."

"Okay, Sandoval," Jonathan said, "I'll pat them on their little fannies and tell them what good players they are."

"No, really, Jonathan. They need to know we believe in them."

"Hey, look, I'll tell Harlan he's doing okay when he *does* do okay. But it's not him I'm worried about. It's those two doofus third graders. They never should have even made this team."

By now the umpire was barking to Jonathan to take one more warmup and then get going.

"Hey, I'm ready to go now," Jonathan yelled to the ump. "I don't need to warm up." He looked at Kenny and added, "I'm *hot*, man. Don't think this game is going to end with you ahead of me in RBIs, either."

Kenny gritted his teeth. As he walked back to his position, he found himself hoping that he'd have players on base when he got up next time.

But Jonathan *was* hot. He threw BBs at the Mariners' batter—their pitcher. The poor kid looked scared. He finally swung and missed for strike three. Kenny didn't think the kid even saw the ball.

But then Cisco, the Mariners' lead-off batter and left fielder, managed to hit a soft grounder to the right side.

Kenny saw the disaster coming.

Ben didn't charge the ball. He stayed back and let the ball bounce toward him.

Even if he had fielded it cleanly, the throw would have been late, but he let the ball slip under his glove.

And then he made another rookie mistake. He spun around, grabbed the ball and tried to throw way too hard. The ball went flying past Jenny.

The runner scooted around to second.

"What an idiot!" Jonathan said, plenty loud enough for Ben to hear.

Kenny shook his head. That wasn't going to help Ben at all.

Jonathan walked back to the mound and fired a pitch that could have sawed a bat in half. But it was low and Harlan let it get under his glove.

Passed ball.

The runner moved to third.

"You've got no one to back you up, Jonny. You're going to have to do it alone," Jonathan's dad shouted. "You better strike this kid out!"

Jonathan nodded, and then he did just that.

Two outs now, and Jonathan still had his shutout.

Cast, the center fielder, lifted a fly to short

right field. It looked like the Dodgers were out of the inning.

Ben was running back for the ball, and Anthony came charging in.

But neither one called for it, and both kept running. And then Anthony and Ben, both at the same time, decided to let the other one make the catch.

The ball dropped between them.

The run scored.

And Jonathan lost his shutout.

"You stupid *idiots!*" he screamed.

Ben and Anthony walked back to their positions. Kenny could see how bad they felt.

Jonathan threw his cap on the grass and then stared out at the two rookies. "We'd have a great team if we didn't have to let you two *boneheads* play," he screamed at them.

★ 4 ★

Bad Vibrations

Coach Wilkens walked onto the field. "Jonathan," he said, firmly, "I'm taking you off the mound. I'd take you out of the game but I've already used the players from the bench."

Jonathan was still out of control. "What are you *talking* about, Coach? Those guys just lost my *shutout*."

Kenny was standing close by. He could still hear the coach when he lowered his voice and said, "Jonathan, that's enough. You keep it up and you're going to be off this team."

The coach waved for Eddie Boschi to come in to pitch.

Then he looked back at Jonathan. "Play left field. But I want to see some sign that you care about this *team*. If I don't see that, I don't want you—no matter how much talent you have."

Jonathan seemed to know he was walking on the edge. He tromped out to left field without saying a word.

Jonathan's dad was the one screaming at Coach Wilkens. He came down to the chain-link fence and shouted, "What do you think you're doing, Coach? Are you trying to *blow* this game?"

Coach Wilkens talked to Eddie Boschi while Mr. Swingle kept hollering. Then the coach walked directly to the fence. He said something to Jonathan's dad that Kenny couldn't hear.

But Mr. Swingle said, loudly, *"No way.* You try to kick him off and I'll have my lawyer on you."

Coach Wilkens walked back to the dugout. He stood next to his son and folded his arms. Kenny knew he meant what he had said. And it scared Kenny. Jonathan had really messed up, but the team did need him.

Eddie Boschi pitched the rest of the game. He gave up three runs, but that wasn't all his fault. The Dodgers no longer seemed to have their hearts—or minds—in the game. Ben and Anthony messed up plenty, but so did the experienced players.

At one point Sterling lobbed a throw to the infield. He assumed the base runner heading for third wouldn't try to score.

He was wrong.

Billy made a throw to second when he had no chance to get the runner. The ball bounced in the dirt and got past Kenny, and the runner got up and jogged on over to third.

The Mariners seemed to gain confidence once Jonathan was not pitching—and once the Dodgers started making mistakes. They played pretty well in the field.

But the Dodgers helped them plenty.

Kenny came up in the fifth with Henry on first. He really wanted to drive that run home and get his third RBI. He swung as hard as he could, but he got under the ball and lifted a pop fly to the left side.

Everyone seemed to be doing the same thing.

All this time, Jonathan wouldn't speak to anyone. He tried to hit homers every time up, but he never got another hit. He even struck out once and then threw his bat at the fence.

The coach made him go get the bat and stack it in the rack. Kenny was afraid Jonathan was going to push the coach too far.

When the game was over, the Dodgers had their first victory. But no one did a lot of celebrating.

The coach talked to the players. He told them they had played well at times, but then he said, "Listen, kids, I *love* baseball. I've loved it all my life. But it's only fun to play when a team works together—like a machine with all the parts fitting right. We all have to pull for each other. That's what it means to be on a team."

The coach looked at Jonathan, but then he looked right at Kenny. Kenny wondered why.

"But anyway, we won. Let's break out the drinks." He told Michael to get the sodas, and most of the kids ran for the van.

But Coach Wilkens asked Jonathan to stay, and he called Mr. Swingle over. They talked for a long time.

Kenny walked home with Jacob and Harlan. They were all sort of worried. "The coach won't really kick Jonathan off the team, will he?" Jacob asked.

"Not yet," Kenny said. "He'll give him another chance."

"I know. But he wouldn't kick him off anyway, would he? I mean, he's our best player."

Harlan said, "He's good, but he doesn't

have any right to talk to the rookies that way. Remember how we felt last year?"

"Sure," Jacob said. "But we weren't *that* bad. Anthony and Ben can't do anything right. I don't know why the coach even picked them for the team."

"I was that bad last year," Harlan said.

But Jacob told him, "No way."

The boys waited for the stoplight before they crossed the street. A woman rolled down her car window and said, "Did the Dodgers win today?"

"Yeah," Jacob said.

"Good. You're going all the way this year. I'm sure of it."

When she drove away, Harlan said, "Wow! That was the mayor."

"Really?" Kenny was amazed. Everyone in Angel Park was the same way, though.

The local paper had run a story that the team had a chance to win the district championship this year.

"The pressure is on," Harlan said as the

boys walked across the street. "Everyone expects us to be great this year."

"We are," Jacob said. "Look how many kids on our team batted over .300 last year. And with Jonathan on our team, *nobody* is going to beat us."

"Yeah, but what if the coach kicks him off?" Harlan asked.

"He won't," Jacob said. "All Jonathan has to do is shut up about the rookies and we'll be the best Angel Park team *ever*."

"We do have a lot of good players," Harlan said. "And some of the teams lost their best players from last year."

"That's right. And we're not rookies anymore. Kenny, you were 2 for 4 today and Harlan was 1 for 2. So was I. We're all batting .500. And we all had RBIs."

"Yeah," Harlan said, "I don't think anyone can beat us this year. Not with the great *fourth graders* leading the way!" He and Jacob gave each other a high five and they both laughed.

But Kenny didn't feel very good about the

game. He wasn't exactly sure why. Something about this year's team worried him. And something inside didn't feel right.

"Just wait until we clean up on the Reds!" Jacob shouted. "We play them on Wednesday."

Kenny smiled. The thought of really wiping out the Reds was too nice not to enjoy.

And gradually Kenny found himself thinking his friends were right. He went home and told his dad not to worry. The Dodgers were going to be *sharp* against the Reds.

Kenny's dad didn't say too much. But Mrs. Sandoval said, "You've got a great team all right. But that Swingle kid could cause you a lot of trouble."

"He just lost his temper," Kenny told her. "But the coach talked to him. He'll be okay."

Mr. Sandoval was reading the paper. He lowered it and looked over the top. "Kenny," he said, "I didn't like what I saw today. I think you need to think about what you were doing."

Kenny knew what his dad was talking about. Teamwork, playing together, playing smart—all that stuff was important.

But did he mean that Kenny had done something wrong?

No. He had had a good game.

Kenny told himself not to worry. He was playing fine, and the team would come together once Jonathan got his attitude straightened out a little.

That's what Kenny was thinking when he took the mound on Wednesday evening. He figured Jonathan would be on his best behavior, and the team would start to click.

"Hey, Sandoval."

Kenny looked over as Jonathan walked toward him. "I didn't use up all six of my innings the other day. So I'm ready to take over if you get in trouble." He grinned.

Kenny didn't think it was funny. "I'll manage all right for myself," he said.

"It's too bad the rules say I can't pitch

every game," Jonathan said. "I haven't lost a game in two years."

Kenny took a warmup pitch.

"Anyway, it doesn't matter." Jonathan grinned again. "The Reds don't look so hot to me. Even you can beat 'em."

Kenny turned his back on Jonathan. He was going to throw some real *heat* tonight— and show this guy that the Dodgers had more than one good pitcher.

Second Season

BOX SCORE, GAME 1

Angel Park Dodgers 11   San Lorenzo Mariners 4

	ab	r	h	rbi		ab	r	h	rbi
Jie 2b	3	1	2	0	Cisco lf	3	2	1	0
White 3b	4	3	2	0	Smagler 2b	2	1	0	0
Sandoval ss	4	2	2	2	Cast cf	2	1	1	1
Swingle p	4	1	1	1	Rodriguez 1b	3	0	2	0
Malone cf	3	3	3	2	Sullivan 3b	2	0	0	0
Roper 1b	4	1	3	1	Korman c	2	0	1	1
Boschi lf	3	0	1	1	Watson rf	2	0	0	0
Bacon c	2	0	0	0	Bernhardt ss	1	0	0	0
Scott rf	2	0	1	2	Klein p	2	0	0	0
Sloan c	1	0	1	1	Rondeau ss	2	0	0	0
Ruiz rf	2	0	0	0	Casper rf	2	0	0	0
Riddle 2b	2	0	0	0	Ford p	1	0	0	0
ttl	34	11	16	10		24	4	5	2

Dodgers	6 2 0 1 2 0—11
Mariners	0 0 2 0 2 0—4

★ 5 ★

Red Rage

One thing hadn't changed for the Reds since last season. Jimmy Gerstein was still leading off. And he still had a big mouth.

But Winter, the big power-hitting catcher, was gone. So was Tovar, their best pitcher.

In fact, Gerstein had been converted to a pitcher, and Kenny had seen him warming up. He looked pretty good.

But right now he was stepping into the batter's box.

"Hey, Sandoval," he yelled. "Give me your best shot. I'm hitting everything this year."

Kenny didn't answer.

But Jonathan did.

"You'll hit the *dirt* when I pitch against you."

"Jonathan!" the coach yelled. "We're not getting that stuff started today. Remember?"

The umpire behind the plate told Jonathan the same thing.

"Okay, okay," Jonathan said.

Kenny made a nice pitch. He fired hard and kept the ball low in the strike zone. Gerstein swung and foul tipped it.

Billy yelled, "Nice pitch, Kenny. Two more like that." He threw the ball back to Kenny.

"Yeah, give me the same pitch and look where it ends up," Gerstein called to Kenny.

The infield talked it up as Kenny got ready for his next pitch. "Strike him out, Kenny," Henry yelled. "Blow it by him." And then everyone started their chant: "Hey, batta, batta, batta, batta. . . . *SWING!!!*"

Kenny knew when he let the ball go that he hadn't followed through. The ball sailed high. Gerstein tomahawked it, and knocked it hard into right field.

Jacob charged, but he had to take the ball on one bounce. Gerstein was on with a single.

Kenny tried not to let that bother him.

Gerstein was jeering at him in a steady stream, but Kenny shut that all out.

He fired a good pitch. Swing and a miss.

The next pitch was a little outside, and this time the batter—the second baseman—fouled it off.

Those first two pitches had had some real power behind them. Now was the time to try the curve.

Kenny took something off the pitch, and it broke down and away. The batter stepped out of his closed stance too early, swung awkwardly . . . and missed.

But Gerstein took off for second. Billy was taken by surprise. He came up firing, but the ball hung in the air, high.

Jonathan covered second. He leaped for

the ball, but it glanced off his glove and bounced into center field.

Gerstein jumped up and raced to third.

That was bad enough, but then he stood on the bag and laughed. "What's the matter, Swingle?" he said. "I thought you were supposed to be pretty good. You can't even catch the ball."

"Oh, yeah?" Jonathan said. "I can outplay you *any* day."

The coach was quick to tell Jonathan to keep quiet, but Jonathan's dad yelled, "Don't let that kid talk to you like that. Tell him to shut his mouth!"

Kenny walked over to Jonathan. "Don't let Gerstein bother you," he said. "He *tries* to make guys mad—so they'll mess up."

"That stuff doesn't bother me," Jonathan said.

Gerstein had never stopped. "Hey, Sandoval, I can spot your curve every time. It's easy to steal on. Throw one now and I'll steal home."

Kenny tried to ignore Gerstein, but he

wondered whether the guy really was picking up his pitches.

Gerstein was working on Jonathan again. "Hey, Swingle, is your hitting just like your fielding?"

Jonathan didn't respond at first, but when Gerstein kept it up, Jonathan finally said, "I batted almost .600 last year. What did you bat?"

Kenny was trying to concentrate. He made a good pitch—hard and at the knees. But the batter, Schulman, spanked the ball fairly hard on the ground, and right at Jonathan.

Jonathan fielded the ball with a sure, smooth motion. Then he came up and hurled the ball . . . into the next county.

Maybe the ball slipped out of his hand. All Kenny knew was that Jenny couldn't have knocked it down with a flagpole.

Gerstein scored and Schulman ended up on second.

And Jonathan was kicking dirt in all directions.

The Reds were loving it. "Hey, Swingle,"

Gerstein yelled, "tell us your batting average again."

"Instead of 'Swat,' they ought to call you 'Swish,'" Schulman shouted from second base. Jonathan stared straight ahead. But then Schulman, the Reds' catcher this year, said, "Maybe the big-city boy isn't so great as he thinks he is."

"Shut up," Jonathan yelled back at him.

"Come over here and shut me up."

"Get him!" Mr. Swingle yelled from the sidelines, and suddenly Jonathan bolted toward Schulman. Kenny darted in the same direction. He grabbed Jonathan before he could jump on Schulman.

But that was all for Jonathan.

The coach came out and took him out of the game. He put Ben Riddle in at shortstop.

Things went downhill fast for the Dodgers after that. Ben tried his best, but he must have made six errors before the day was over.

Gerstein turned out not to be so tough.

The Dodgers scored six runs off him. But the Dodgers were a disaster.

The Reds didn't beat the Dodgers.

The Dodgers beat the Dodgers.

They gave up eleven runs, and most of them were on mistakes. And a lot of the mistakes were mental: missing the cutoff man on throws from the outfield; losing track of the number of outs; not watching runners closely enough.

Late in the game, Coach Wilkens put Jonathan back in the game. He got a hit and drove in a run. But he was still *very* mad. He wouldn't say a word to anyone.

When the game was over and the Reds had finished their gloating and had left, Coach Wilkens had his players sit on the grass.

Jonathan wouldn't even sit by the other kids. And his dad was standing not far off, his jaw set tight. Kenny figured Mr. Swingle was ready to have it out with the coach.

"All right, now listen," Coach Wilkens said. He didn't sound mad, but he sounded stern.

"I've heard all the talk I want to hear about batting averages and RBIs. That stuff happened last year; it doesn't mean a thing now."

He paced back and forth in front of the players. "I don't mind a team losing when kids play hard and play smart. But when you come out to the park and expect to win because you've read in the paper how good you are—well, that makes me upset."

He pointed at Jonathan. "Jonathan, you're a fine player. But all you care about is running up your own numbers. You start playing as part of this team or you're gone. I'd rather take last place and coach kids who want to play together. I want you to stop mouthing off and start *playing ball.*"

Jonathan didn't say a word.

But his dad did.

"Hey, what about the Reds? They started all the trouble."

"Mr. Swingle, I care what *our* team does. And if I hear you yelling any more abuse, I'm going to ask the umpire to have you leave the park. According to Little League rules, unsportsmanlike conduct is not allowed by the fans—especially the parents."

Kenny watched Mr. Swingle. He came within a breath of saying more. But something kept him from doing it. Maybe he knew the coach was right.

The coach paused and looked around, and then he said, "Kids, when I was your age I used to watch guys like Willie Mays, Mickey Mantle, Hank Aaron. They were my heroes, and they all had big numbers on their baseball cards. But it was a thing of beauty to watch those men play."

Kenny watched the coach. He seemed to be struggling to think exactly what he wanted to say.

"Somehow, you've got to get the idea of what we're trying to do here. I want you to learn this great game. Yelling smart stuff at the other team—that's ugly. That's childish. Speak with your bats and your gloves. That's what *real* athletes do. That's what all the great players have done."

The coach looked right at Kenny. "You've all got to think about what you're doing out there. You've got to decide you're on a *team.*"

Kenny was amazed. Why was the coach looking at him?

But then he said, "All right, let's go celebrate."

Celebrate? Kenny was taken by surprise.

But the coach was nodding. "Maybe we learned a lesson tonight. Maybe we needed to get this game out of the way so we can be the team we want to be."

And so the Dodgers tried to celebrate. They drank root beer and they gradually cheered up a little. Kenny had the feeling that the players had taken the coach's words to heart.

And Kenny did notice one thing that pleased him: Jonathan wasn't talking. He seemed to be thinking things over.

Only one thing still troubled Kenny. He couldn't think why the coach had looked at *him* that way.

BOX SCORE, GAME 2

Cactus Hills Reds 11

	ab	r	h	rbi
Gerstein p	3	3	2	0
Trulis 2b	2	3	1	0
Schulman c	2	2	1	1
Rutter 3b	2	1	0	0
Lum ss	1	1	1	1
Young lf	3	0	2	2
Bonthuis 1b	4	0	0	0
Higdon rf	2	0	0	0
Harrison cf	2	1	1	0
Hileman rf	1	0	0	0
Alfini cf	1	0	0	0
Charles 1b	1	0	0	0
ttl	**24**	**11**	**8**	**4**

Angel Park Dodgers 6

	ab	r	h	rbi
Jie 2b	4	0	2	1
White 3b	4	1	1	0
Sandoval p	4	1	1	0
Swingle ss	1	0	1	1
Malone cf	2	0	0	0
Roper 1b	3	1	2	2
Boschi lf	2	1	1	0
Bacon c	1	0	0	0
Scott rf	2	1	1	1
Riddle ss	2	0	0	0
Sloan c	1	1	0	0
Ruiz rf	1	0	0	0
	27	**6**	**9**	**5**

Reds   2 0 5   2 0 2—11
Dodgers 2 0 0   4 0 0—6

★ 6 ★

Benched

Kenny thought a lot about the coach's words, and he asked his dad what he thought.

"I think you have to figure that out for yourself," his dad told him. "But I will say this. I don't think Jonathan is the only one who has to get his head straightened out."

"I know that," Kenny said. He was sitting on his bed, in his room, and his dad was leaning against the closed door. "We were all playing bad."

"That's not what I'm talking about."

"What do you mean then?"

Mr. Sandoval smiled. "Well, I don't like to give speeches. I want you to think about it yourself. But I heard what the coach said to you, and I agree."

Dad left.

Kenny still didn't understand.

But by Saturday morning Kenny had his mind made up that he was going to play his heart out. If Jonathan pitched, Kenny would be pulling for him. And he would pull for the third graders when they got in the game.

Kenny was a team player; he was sure of it.

And then . . . the coach turned everything upside down.

He announced the starting lineup: Ben was *starting* at shortstop. Anthony was in right field. Eddie was pitching.

And on the bench: Jonathan, Billy, . . . and Kenny.

The coach didn't say why. He just announced the team and told everyone to play *as a team*. "I want to hear everyone supporting everyone else out there today," he told them.

And so the Dodgers took the field. And Kenny walked into the dugout and sat down.

When Jonathan got there, he was mad, but he wasn't saying anything. Maybe he knew better.

Or maybe he was trying hard to do the right thing.

Billy was mad, too. "What's the coach getting on me for? I didn't do anything." He glanced at Jonathan, as if to say, "You're the one who caused the trouble."

The three boys sat down on the bench. They said very little.

After a few minutes the coach walked to the dugout and said, "Boys, I'm not punishing you. I just want you to sit here and think for a while. And I want you to support the players out on the field."

"Aren't we going to play?" Billy asked.

"Yeah, you'll play. Everyone plays." He put his hands on his hips. "You three players are crucial to this team. And you're *good* players. But you need to think about what you've been doing so far this season."

Kenny was stunned. He knew that Jonathan had been making a fool of himself. And Billy had a big mouth. But he couldn't think of anything he'd done wrong himself. Why had the coach included *him?*

Then Kenny heard Mr. Swingle say, "Jonny, what's going on?"

Jonathan got up and walked to the end of the dugout. He and his dad talked for quite some time. Kenny could hear angry voices. But finally Mr. Swingle went back to the bleachers.

Kenny watched as Eddie made his first pitch. It was hard not to wish that some of the kids would mess up and the coach would have to put his *best* players in the game.

The pitch was a strike. Eddie looked confident too. All the guys in the infield were really talking it up. They seemed to have their minds made up that they were going to play better than last time.

Another strike!

Eddie was throwing harder this year, and

he seemed to have his motion under better control.

He came with another good fastball and the batter swung and missed.

Eddie actually got a strikeout.

The next batter, the center fielder, ticked a ball that rolled out in front of the plate. Harlan jumped on it and made a good throw to first.

The Dodgers were already looking better than they had against the Reds.

And then the next batter hit a solid grounder to shortstop. Ben tried to get down on the ball, the way the coach had taught him to do. But he was awkward—and he seemed scared. The ball skipped up his arm and over his shoulder.

Ben spun, grabbed the ball, and made a late throw to first. Jenny had to come off the bag to catch it.

Billy laughed. "The coach is getting what he wants, I guess," he said.

But Jonathan didn't say anything.

All the Dodger players were yelling to Ben not to worry. And Henry White trotted over and talked to him. Ben nodded, and Kenny knew that Henry was telling him that he would be okay.

Eddie also got tough with the next batter. He got ahead of him, 0 and 2, and then he used one of his off-speed pitches. It broke over the plate for a called strike three.

Kenny was impressed. What had happened to Eddie?

The Dodgers hustled back to the bench. "Good job, Eddie," they were all yelling. No one said anything to the guys on the bench.

Kenny was getting excited. But he still couldn't think what the coach wanted from him.

Lian started things off right with a walk, and Henry came through with a sharp single to left field. But Jenny hit a line drive right at the second baseman and Malone lifted an easy fly to center field.

Eddie came up with a runner still at third.

He took a good swing, but he bounced a grounder to the first baseman.

No runs for the Dodgers.

And that's how things went again in the second inning. The Dodgers got the A's out easily, and they got a runner on when Jacob hit a double. They left him there, however, when Harlan, Ben, and Anthony were all easy outs.

Still, the team charged back to the field, and they were yelling to each other that they were going to get some runs next inning.

They seemed to be sure they could come through.

Then the trouble started.

The A's slow-running right fielder hit an easy grounder to shortstop. Ben had all the time in the world, but he took his eye off the ball and let it bounce off his glove.

At least he didn't make another wild throw.

But Anthony made up for that on the next play.

For the first time a batter hit a fly to right. Anthony charged in on it and then saw it whistle over his head. He threw on the brakes, turned around and lumbered after it, but the ball rolled all the way to the fence.

Sterling beat Anthony to the ball, but by the time he made the throw, the batter had circled the bases for an inside-the-park homer.

Or a four-base error.

And things didn't get much better after that. The next batter hit a line drive for a single, and the kid after that hit another ground ball to Ben.

Another error.

By the time it was all over, the A's were ahead 5 to 0.

Billy was fuming. "How long is the coach going to let this go on?" he asked Jonathan.

But Jonathan didn't answer. In fact, he got up and told the players who were returning to the dugout, "Come on! We can still win this thing." And then he told Lian, who was about to lead off, "Get it going. You can do it."

"Don't worry," Lian said, and he was smiling. "We're still going to beat these guys."

Thinking Straight

All the Dodgers were picking up the cheer from Jonathan.

"Come on!" Sterling shouted. "Let's show these guys what we can do. Lian, get it going!"

He walked along in front of the players, clapping his hands. He was a strong, athletic-looking boy, who wore his hair shaved on the sides and square on top. He was a great player but he usually didn't say much. Maybe he sensed that the team needed a leader right now.

"Get on base!" Jenny called to Lian. "We'll bring you around."

Jenny always spoke plenty with her bat,

and she was someone everyone liked. But Kenny thought maybe she was deciding that as a sixth grader, it was time for her to show some leadership too.

Lian smiled and nodded and walked to the batter's box. And he played it smart. The A's pitcher had been staying outside a lot, and the Dodgers had been too eager.

But Lian waited until the pitcher got behind 2 and 0 and brought in a pitch over the plate. He looped a little drive over the second baseman's head for a single.

Billy jumped up and yelled, "Way to go, Lian! Now let's keep it going."

Kenny suddenly wondered what he was doing sitting down. He jumped up, too. "Let's *do it*, Henry!" he yelled. "Let's get these guys."

White took a couple of pitches, and then—*bam!*—he laced a ball into center.

He stopped at first and yelled back to the other players, "Come on, now. Let's keep it going!"

Two on. Runners at first and second.

Now Jonathan was up and yelling, "Come on, Jenny! We can do it. Get a little bingo."

Jenny kept her promise. She waited for a good pitch and pulled it hard into right field. Lian scored and Henry went to third.

A run in. Two on. Still no outs.

Things were looking up.

Everyone was cheering, and Jonathan was as excited as anyone. "Come on, we can do it!" he kept shouting.

Sterling then clouted the ball hard, and for a moment it seemed that the Dodgers were going to catch up fast. But the ball stayed in the park and the left fielder made a good catch.

Henry tagged up and scored, but now there was an out.

Then Eddie chopped a grounder to third that looked like a possible out. The third baseman took the ball on a high hop and tried to go to second for the force. But Jenny slid hard and the third baseman's throw pulled the second baseman off the bag.

It was close, but the woman who was um-piring in the field barked, *"Saaa-eeef!!!!"*

Jacob was coming up.

Kenny was pulling for him, but he wanted to get in the game himself. The bottom of the batting order was coming up and three of the best hitters were sitting on the bench!

And suddenly the luck changed.

Jacob hit a hard shot toward left field. The shortstop dove for the ball and couldn't get it, but it bounced off his glove and rolled toward third.

The third baseman picked it up and had no time for a throw. But he dove at Jenny, who was running toward third. He almost missed her, but he touched her foot as it kicked up behind.

"Oooooo-uuuuut!!!!"

Jenny slid into third and then hopped up. "What?" she yelled.

"He got you on the foot," the umpire said.

Jenny hadn't felt the tag. She walked back to the dugout with her hands on her hips and her head shaking.

"It's okay," Coach Wilkens yelled to her. "I think he *did* tag you."

So now there were two outs.

Harlan was coming up. He was hitting pretty well, but Kenny knew that Billy was still a tougher out at a time like this.

"Come on, Harlan!" Jonathan yelled. "Show what you can do."

"Time out!" the coach yelled, and he walked toward the dugout. "Are you guys ready to play now?"

"Yeah!!!!" they all three yelled at the same time.

"Do you understand why I had you sit down?"

Billy was first to answer. "You don't like it when I brag and mouth off to the other team—and stuff like that."

"Well, there's more to it than that," the coach said.

Jonathan said, "You want us pulling for each other."

"I don't want to hear any more about individual stats all year," Coach Wilkens said.

"Do you understand that? The only stat that counts is 'team wins' and 'team losses.'"

"Okay," Jonathan said.

Kenny knew that was the right answer. He also knew how hard that would be for Jonathan.

"All right," Coach Wilkens said. "Billy, you go in for Harlan, and Jonathan, you'll bat next, for Ben."

Then he looked at Kenny. "Kenny, do you understand why I put you on the bench?"

"Well, I . . . don't know. I always pull for the team. And I wasn't mouthing off or—"

"Okay. Sit down. You do a little more thinking. I'll talk to you in a minute."

Billy was walking to the batter's box. Jonathan—the one who had caused all the trouble—was going out to find a bat. Kenny couldn't believe it. He was still benched.

He sat down, and he tried to think. But mostly his mind was spinning. It was Jonathan who was talking about his stats. And he was the one getting on the new players. Kenny hadn't done any of that.

But just then Kenny heard the *CRACK* of a bat. Billy had hit a long fly in the right-center gap. Runners were powering around the bases.

Eddie scored.

Jacob scored.

Billy rounded second, and then he threw on the brakes and went back to second.

He might have made it. But the coach had put on the red light. The Dodgers still needed another run to tie the game. Getting thrown out at third would only end the rally.

Kenny remembered that Billy had run right on past a "stop" signal in the last game, without watching the coach. This time he didn't let that happen.

But Kenny couldn't think what *he* had done wrong in the last game. He hadn't played his best. His pitching could have been sharper, but the coach wouldn't get on him about that. Sure, he had wanted to show Jonathan a thing or two—but he hadn't *said* anything.

Jonathan was stepping up to bat. Kenny was angry. The guy had been a jerk, had gotten himself pulled off the mound for being so hard on Ben and Anthony, and then he had almost slugged a guy. Kenny hadn't done one thing wrong.

And yet, here Jonathan was in the game.

Jonathan let a high pitch go by. He seemed to be concentrating hard.

"Come on, Swat," the players were all yelling.

And Kenny heard Mr. Swingle yell, "Drive in that run, Jonny. Knock the ball out of here."

Kenny wasn't yelling. He was trying to think what he could tell the coach.

The next pitch was in the strike zone and Jonathan took a nice stroke and drove the ball into right field.

It was a solid hit, and it scored the run.

The game was tied.

As the throw came home, Jonathan rounded first. For a moment he seemed ready to take a chance on making it to second. But he stopped and went back.

And that wasn't like Jonathan. He loved to show off his speed. This time, however, he had used some judgment.

"Kenny!"

"Yeah?" Kenny started for the dugout door.

But the coach said, "Now, tell me. Do you know why you've been sitting down?"

Kenny knew he had to say something. "I guess I . . . maybe could have played a little harder."

The coach stared at him for several seconds, and then he said, "Go ahead, Anthony. Stay in the game. Let's keep this rally going."

★ 8 ★

Getting Together

===========================

Kenny felt sick.

And mad.

It didn't make sense. Anthony struck out and that was the end of the rally.

Jared Oshima, the A's quick second baseman, was stepping up to the plate. He waved his bat around—the way Coach Wilkens told the players not to do—but he socked a double in the left-center gap.

Maybe the Dodgers hadn't taken over the momentum of the game quite yet.

Eddie seemed to let the hit bother him. He threw four straight balls to the second batter.

Jonathan was playing shortstop. He yelled

to Eddie, "Don't try to throw too hard. The ball is sailing on you."

Eddie nodded and took the advice. He got the ball down again and the batter rolled a ground ball straight to Henry at third. Henry tagged the bag and tried to make the throw to first, but he missed the double play by half a step.

Jonathan yelled to Henry, "Great play!" And then he made a great one of his own. The chubby catcher hit a blooper into left field. Jonathan ran—all out—to catch up to the ball, and made a lunging catch with his back to home plate.

When the next batter hit a pop-up straight in the air, Billy handled it and the Dodgers were out of the inning.

The score was still tied, 5 to 5.

Kenny watched Jonathan as he ran toward the dugout. He was yelling to Billy about his good catch.

But Kenny had to wonder. Jonathan hadn't acted like this before. How come the big change all of a sudden?

Jonathan came straight to Kenny, and he

said, "Come here a sec." He took Kenny's arm and sort of pulled him to the end of the dugout. "Come on, Kenny," he said. "We need you. Tell the coach you were going for the stats, the same as me."

"But I wasn't."

Jonathan laughed. "Kenny, I'm cocky, but at least I know it."

"So how come you're the big team player all of a sudden?"

"What difference does it make? It's what you have to do if you want to play."

Kenny couldn't believe it. "You mean this is just a big act?"

"Look, just do it. Tell him you want to be a team player, and he'll let you play." Jonathan walked away.

Kenny followed him. "Is that what you were doing? Just faking it?"

Jonathan didn't answer for a moment, but then he said, "Look, Kenny, my dad yells at me to get shutouts and knock home runs. And the coach tells me to forget about the stats. What am I supposed to do? It's the coach who decides who plays."

"I know but—"

"Kenny . . ." But Jonathan struggled to find the words. "It's more fun the coach's way. It's better. I tried to be on the team last inning—and I liked it. It felt good."

"Hey, I know that. But I wasn't the one bragging about RBIs and all that stuff."

"Maybe not. But you wanted to beat me."

Kenny didn't answer. He couldn't really deny that.

Lian was leading off again. And he came through one more time. He delivered another soft single to right field, as though he could do it every time.

"See what Lian does," Jonathan said. "He knows he can't hit homers so he gets on base any way he can. And then he plays great defense. He wins games."

"Look, you don't have to tell me all that. I know it."

Kenny got up. "Come on, Henry. Get a hit!" he shouted.

Henry took a sweet swing. He delivered another hit.

Henry wasn't like Jonathan. He went out and played great games, but he never bragged.

And that's how Kenny was, too.

The coach knew that.

And yet . . . something wasn't quite right. Kenny knew how he had felt after the first two games. He tried to think what had been wrong.

Jenny was up now. She played it smart, as usual. She watched the strike zone and waited for her pitch. When she didn't get it, she took the walk and loaded the bases.

Kenny thought about the bad pitches he had swung at in the second game.

He even thought he knew why he had taken those swings.

Bases loaded. Things looked good again.

Sterling hit a hard shot that almost took the second baseman's glove off.

But the kid held on, and he flipped the ball to first. Jenny had broken for second, thinking the ball was going through, and she couldn't get back.

She was doubled off base.

And then Eddie hit a fly-ball out.

That was that. The score was still tied.

And Kenny was still on the bench.

But the coach had to put him in now. That was the rule. Everyone had to play six defensive outs and bat once.

"Anthony, good job," Coach Wilkens yelled. "I'm putting Kenny in now."

But he stopped Kenny before he could run onto the field. "Do you understand yet?"

"Well . . ." Kenny still hadn't said it to himself. "I guess I got into a contest with Jonathan."

"What did you do that you wouldn't normally do?"

Kenny took a long breath. "In the first game, I came up with Henry on first, and instead of trying to move him over, I swung for the fence—so I could get an RBI."

"Yup. I saw it. So did your dad. He and I talked about it. But it wasn't just the first game. Your dad and I didn't like what we saw in the second game either. That's when he told me I ought to let you sit on the bench and think for a few innings."

Kenny knew what the coach meant. And he had to admit to himself now that he had really known all along. "In that second game I kept swinging at bad pitches because I wanted RBIs, not walks."

"All right. That's exactly right. Get in the game. You're going to be better than ever, Kenny. Better than ever." Coach Wilkens slapped Kenny on the shoulder, and Kenny ran out to play left field.

The coach moved Jacob to right, where he normally played.

That turned out to be a wise move. On the first batter, Kenny used his speed to run down a fly that Jacob never would have caught.

The Dodgers then got the A's in order.

The score was still tied.

Jacob led off the bottom of the fifth. But this time he didn't come through. He topped the ball and grounded out.

Billy had trouble too. He got behind in the count and then swung at a bad pitch. Another grounder, another out.

"Swat" was coming up, and Kenny knew

he was probably thinking long ball by now. One big swing could do it.

That's what the A's were thinking too. The outfielders moved back. The infield gave some ground.

But Jonathan surprised everyone in the park by dropping a perfect bunt along the third-base line. He ran it out easily and then yelled to Kenny to move him around.

Kenny knew what he had to do: keep the inning going. Get the runner in scoring position.

He knew he could punch the ball to the right side—the same as Lian—and move the speedy Jonathan all the way to third.

So Kenny took a smooth stroke and poked the ball to right.

But he got all of it.

The ball shot off his bat and kept going.

For one terrible moment, as the right fielder jumped in the air, Kenny thought he had hit the ball too hard and just made a big, loud out.

And then he realized that the ball was

not in the right fielder's glove. It was
GONE!!!

Over the right field fence for a *HOME
RUN!!!*

And as it turned out, that's all the Dodgers
needed. Eddie got the A's out in the sixth
and it was all over.

The Dodgers had won 7 to 5.

This time the Dodgers did some real celebrating. And Kenny had the feeling that
the latest edition of the Dodgers had just
become a team.

But there was something he had to tell
the coach. "I wasn't swinging for the fence
that time. I just—"

"Hey, I know that," the coach said, and
he laughed. "That's how most homers are
hit. You have quick wrists, Kenny. You drive
the ball hard. When a batter tries to muscle
up, he uses his arms and shoulders, and he
takes his wrists out of action. That's why you
get the best numbers when you don't try for
them."

Kenny nodded. He understood.

As he turned to walk away, Jonathan was waiting. "Great job, Kenny," he said.

And Kenny was pretty sure he meant it.

And then Kenny took off. He told Jacob and Harlan he would be right back. But first he wanted to talk to someone.

He ran toward his parents, who were waiting on the sidelines.

"Dad, thanks!" Kenny yelled, as he ran toward him.

"For what?" Mr. Sandoval said.

"You know for what. For telling the coach to bench me!"

Mr. Sandoval laughed, but Kenny leaped right on him and hugged him with both arms and both legs.

And when he got down, Jacob and Harlan were waiting for their traditional three-way leaping high five.

"We're going all the way now!" Jacob shouted. "We're *superstars!!!*"

But Harlan clapped a hand over his mouth and Kenny said, "No more of that! Let's just try to win our next game!"

BOX SCORE, GAME 3

Paseo A's 5					Angel Park Dodgers 7				
	ab	r	h	rbi		ab	r	h	rbi
Oshima 2b	4	1	2	0	Jie 2b	2	1	2	0
De Klein cf	1	1	0	0	White 3b	3	1	3	0
Sullivan lf	2	1	1	0	Roper 1b	3	0	1	1
Smith c	2	0	0	1	Malone cf	3	0	0	1
Santos 1b	3	0	1	2	Boschi p	3	1	1	0
Chavez ss	3	0	0	0	Scott lf	3	1	1	0
Powell 3b	2	0	1	0	Sloan c	1	0	0	0
Trout rf	1	1	0	0	Riddle ss	1	0	0	0
Watrous p	3	1	1	1	Ruiz rf	2	0	0	0
Henegan 3b	1	0	0	0	Bacon c	2	1	1	2
Naile rf	1	0	0	0	Swingle ss	2	1	2	1
Reilly cf	1	0	0	0	Sandoval lf	1	1	1	2
ttl	**24**	**5**	**6**	**4**		**26**	**7**	**12**	**7**

A's   0 0 5 0 0 0—5
Dodgers 0 0 5 0 2 x—7

Second Season

League standings after three games:

Giants	3–0
Padres	2–1
Dodgers	2–1
Reds	2–1
Mariners	0–3
A's	0–3

First game scores:

Dodgers	11	Mariners	4
Reds	6	A's	4
Giants	7	Padres	6

Second game scores:

Reds	11	Dodgers	6
Padres	9	A's	2
Giants	14	Mariners	1

Third game scores:

Dodgers	7	A's	5
Giants	10	Reds	6
Padres	6	Mariners	3

LIAN JIE *

At-bats	Runs	Hits	RBIs	Avg.
5	1	3	2	.600

* Jie only played in four games.

HENRY WHITE

At-bats	Runs	Hits	RBIs	Avg.
72	26	37	15	.514

JENNY ROPER

At-bats	Runs	Hits	RBIs	Avg.
44	16	21	16	.477

FIRST-YEAR STATISTICS

KENNY SANDOVAL

At-bats	Runs	Hits	RBIs	Avg.
73	23	34	30	.466

JACOB SCOTT

At-bats	Runs	Hits	RBIs	Avg.
28	9	11	8	.393

STERLING MALONE

At-bats	Runs	Hits	RBIs	Avg.
59	14	22	22	.373

HARLAN SLOAN

At-bats	Runs	Hits	RBIs	Avg.
27	9	10	10	.370

FIRST-YEAR STATISTICS

BILLY BACON

At-bats	Runs	Hits	RBIs	Avg.
52	17	17	16	.326

EDDIE BOSCHI

At-bats	Runs	Hits	RBIs	Avg.
60	11	15	8	.250

ALL-STAR OF THE MONTH

STERLING MALONE

Sterling Malone is a sixth grader this year and one of the real leaders of the Angel Park All-Stars. Tall for his age and very strong, he has used his size and his strength to hit some long home runs. But he is also very fast, and for that reason he plays the speed position in the outfield, center field. He's a sure-handed fielder who can run a long way for the ball and who can make spectacular catches for a twelve-year-old.

But hitting is where Sterling has really made his mark. He was a good hitter in his fifth-grade year, batting .373, but he has hit even better in the first half of this season, batting .448. Lately, he has been on an amazing hot streak. In the last six games he has batted .526.

Sterling not only hits well, he also comes through with runners on base. He was second in runs batted in last season, with 22. He has more than matched that pace this season, with 12 RBIs in the first half.

The best baseball players can hit, field, and throw, but they offer something more than that to a team. What Sterling gives to the Dodgers is strong, even leadership. He's not excitable—not a "cheerleader"—but he is confident, and he spreads a positive attitude through the team. He is friendly and supportive of the other players, and he's one of the first to teach younger players the techniques he has learned. When players on other teams shout insults, Sterling has a quiet way of showing them up with his bat or his glove, not with his mouth.

And when he's in the classroom, Sterling shows everyone up with that good mind of his. He's a very bright boy, and he reads a lot, but he's especially interested in anything having to do with airplanes. His father is a former Air Force pilot who now flies commercial airplanes. Sterling has built dozens of model airplanes, which practically fill his bedroom. His goal is to follow his father's footsteps and become a pilot, but he would also like to go one more step and become an astronaut. He doesn't really like math very much, but his dad says he's going to have to be a good math student to make his goal, and so Sterling works hard on all his subjects, even the ones he doesn't like.

One of the good things about having a pilot for a father is getting free airline tickets. Sterling's family has been to Hawaii and the Bahamas, as well as all around the United States. This coming year they plan to take a trip to Europe. Sterling thinks that's great, but he wants to make the trip at a time when he won't miss any part of one of his sports seasons. For a kid who plays as many sports as Sterling does, that won't be easy! There's baseball from March through September. And then, of course, soccer in the fall. Basketball in winter and early spring. Tennis, as much as he can, in between his other sports. . . .

DEAN HUGHES has written many books for children, including the popular *Nutty* stories and *Jelly's Circus*. He has also published such works of literary fiction for young adults as the highly acclaimed *Family Pose*. Writing keeps Mr. Hughes very busy, but he does find time to run and play golf—and he loves to watch almost all sports. His home is in Utah. He and his wife have three children, all in college.

READ THESE OTHER ANGE

"A thoroughly enjoyable series."
—*Publishers Weekly*

#1 MAKING THE TEAM

Kenny, Harlan, and Jacob have officially made the team, but some of the older players—mostly team bully Rodney Bunson—seem bent on making life miserable for the three rookies. Can the third-grade Little Leaguers stand up to some big-league bullying?

#2 BIG BASE HIT

Awkward and big for his age, Harlan seems to do everything wrong—and it's making him wonder whether he really belongs on the team at all. But then the pitcher throws the ball, and Harlan gives the team just what they've all been waiting for: a big base hit!

#3 WINNING STREAK

Kenny's in a slump—and it spells big trouble for the undefeated Angel Park Dodgers. Jacob's got a few tricks that he thinks will help, but his wacky ideas only seem to make matters worse. Then he hits on the one trick that puts Kenny back in action, just in time to put the team back on a winning streak!

#4 WHAT A CATCH!

Brian desperately wants to make his last season in Little League his best ever, but his mistakes might cost the team the championship. The All-Stars try to help their nervous friend build his self-confidence, but it takes a pep talk from a major-league pro to get Brian back on track.

RK ALL-STARS BY DEAN HUGHES

#5 ROOKIE STAR

Does Kenny think he's too good for his old friends? He's been seen practicing with some older players, and the local paper runs an article calling him a "rookie star." Jacob and Harlan think he's got a bad case of swollen head, and the whole team starts fighting. Can they get it together before it's too late?

#6 PRESSURE PLAY

Their rivals are playing dirty and the Dodgers are starting to lose their spirit as well as their tempers. Jacob, benched because of slipping grades, sees that it's up to him to use his brains instead of his bat to come up with a solution that will put the Dodgers back in the running for the championship. But how?

#7 LINE DRIVE

When the Dodgers' second baseman breaks his leg, no one expects that Coach Wilkens will choose little Lian Jie, a new player from the minor league, to take his place. Harlan can see that Lian Jie's got the right stuff to be a Dodger, but how can he help the new kid prove it to the rest of the team?

#8 CHAMPIONSHIP GAME

The Dodgers have a shot at the league title, but they're puzzled by Coach Wilkens's strange behavior. First he takes star slugger Rodney Bunson out of the game, and then he starts coaching players on other teams. Can the Dodgers keep their coach from wrecking their chances at the championship?

BULLSEYE BOOKS PUBLISHED BY ALFRED A. KNOPF, INC.